Hurry Up, Ilua!

By Nola Helen Hicks

Published by Inhabit Media Inc.
www.inhabitmedia.com

Inhabit Media Inc. (Iqaluit) P.O. Box 11125, Iqaluit, Nunavut, X0A 1H0
(Toronto) 146A Orchard View Blvd., Toronto, Ontario, M4R 1C3

Edited by Louise Flaherty and Neil Christopher
Coloring by Astrid Arijanto

We acknowledge the financial support of the Government of Canada through the Department
of Canadian Heritage Canada Book Fund.

We acknowledge the support of the Canada Council for the Arts for our publishing program.

Printed in Canada.

Canadian Patrimoine
Heritage canadien

Canadä

Canada Council   Conseil des Arts
for the Arts   du Canada

Library and Archives Canada Cataloguing in Publication

Hicks, Nola Helen, 1980-, author, illustrator   Hurry up, Ilua! / by Nola Helen Hicks.

ISBN 978-1-77227-003-7 (pbk.)

        I. Title.

PS8615.I3555H87 2015   jC813'.6   C2015-900480-2

Hurry Up, Ilua!

By Nola Helen Hicks

Ilua lay back on the land while slowly eating some berries from her pocket. She watched the crowds of siksiks rushing by. Berries were being put into baskets, Arctic cotton was being picked, and grass was being gathered. Ilua wondered why everyone was speeding around, since the Long Sleep was more than an hour away.

Ilua knew she would be sleeping underground for the next seven months, and she wanted to enjoy her last moments in the sunshine. Ilua's mother scurried over holding Ilua's little sister, Ivavaa, in her arms.

"I need help with your sister because I am busy getting ready," Ilua's mother said in a hurry. "Here, turn around."

Ilua's mother slid Ivavaa into the back of Ilua's amauti.

"Everyone will go down into the den in one hour for the Long Sleep feast, Ilua. Do not be late. You can't lag behind today, like you do on other days, because we need your help!"

Ilua's mother kissed her and Ivavaa before she rushed away.

"Hi, Lua," said Ivavaa. She pointed to the grey blizzard clouds moving ever closer, saying, "Big cu-wowds."

"Yes," Ilua said, "but we have plenty of time. Let's go gather some Arctic cotton down by the lake to make our beds soft. I would like a fresh drink, too, before the snow falls."

Ilua squeezed her sister's warm little paw and gave her a grin.

The two sisters slowly walked down to the lake as Ivavaa chatted about things that babies like to talk about. Ilua picked cotton and slowly passed the pieces to her sister, who filled up the back of the amauti. Ilua found some lichen, too, and carefully filled her pocket. Ilua crouched down at the edge of the lake and tested the coolness of the water with her paw a few times before sleepily scooping up a cool drink.

Suddenly, a snowflake landed on Ilua's nose. She gasped and jumped up, making Ivavaa giggle.

"Oh no," cried Ilua. "I've taken too long and the snow has started! We have to get back, Ivavaa."

"Yup. I sweepy," said Ivavaa as she rubbed her eyes.

"Someone is ready for the Long Sleep," Ilua laughed.

But her smile turned into a frown as more snow fell. She had to hurry.

As Ilua started back toward her den, the wind began to blow. She could not see the land in front of her. Ilua closed her amauti around her head to cover her sister. She felt Ivavaa snuggle down, and she was glad the back of her amauti was filled with the warm cotton they had picked. Ilua remembered an entrance to her den that was very close to where they stood. She wiped snow from her eyes and squinted through the heavy snowfall. Ilua's den had thirty ways in, but she couldn't see past the snow!

Just then, Ilua saw black wings flapping in the blizzard. A raven landed before her. "Are you lost?" the raven asked, as he turned his head to one side.

"I can't seem to find my way back to the den. I need to get back there quickly before the Long Sleep begins. Can you help me?"

Ilua looked hopefully at the raven as she dug in her pocket. She gave a handful of berries to the raven.

"I will fly around to see if I can find an entrance to your den," said the raven.

He nodded, flew around, and came back to Ilua.

"Sorry. No luck. Be careful!" the raven said, before he blew off into the swirling white storm.

Ilua walked a little farther, aiming for what she thought was home. She put her head down against the wind and pushed forward. Out of nowhere, Ilua bumped into a mound of soft, white fur with a thud.

An Arctic hare twitched her nose and asked, "Are you lost?"

"Yes," said Ilua. "Can you help me find my den? I'll share my lichen with you."

The hare agreed and darted around. But she quickly returned.

"Sorry. No luck. Be careful!" With a worried look, the hare bounced off into the blizzard.

Ilua walked even farther. The blizzard was gusting all around her, and walking was becoming hard. Ilua sniffed as a tear ran down her face. She didn't want to lag behind anymore. She would never delay when her family needed her ever again. Ilua wished she were cuddling with her sister in her soft bed for the Long Sleep. She should have listened to her mother and hurried home.

Then, suddenly, out of the blizzard came a big wolf. Ilua was scared. She felt Ivavaa snore and push against her back as she slept. Ilua had to think fast to keep her sister safe.

"Hello, Wolf," Ilua said, as bravely as she could. "I am lost. Can you use your nose to help me find my den? My community is nearby, but I can't find the hole to the den because of the snow." Ilua smiled and blinked at the wolf, hoping he would help.

The wolf agreed, thinking that an entire community of siksiks would make a fine meal for his pack. He licked his lips and swiftly raced around. Ilua tried hard to keep up, but because she was used to moving so slowly, it was very tiring. Through the falling snow, Ilua could see the wolf's tail. When the tail stopped, Ilua held her breath. The wolf began to dig.

As soon as Ilua saw the opening to her den uncovered by the wolf, she grabbed the Arctic cotton from her hood and threw it at the wolf's eyes. While the wolf could not see, Ilua quickly slipped down the hole and into the den. Ilua ran as fast as she could. The wolf was too big to follow her into the small tunnels.

Ilua ran to her family, told them her story, and warned them of the wolf. Ilua promised that from that day on she would listen to her mother and she would not move slowly when her family needed her. After the feast, Ilua hurried to bed and finally snuggled down with Ivavaa for the Long Sleep.

Pronunciation Guide

amauti—a parka worn by women and girls, pronounced "a-mow-tee."

Ilua—pronounced "e-low-wa."

Ivavaa—pronounced "e-vah-vaah."

siksik—an Arctic ground squirrel, pronounced "sick-sick."

Nola Helen Hicks

is a teacher, writer, and artist living in Chesterfield Inlet, Nunavut. She holds degrees in English literature and education, and loves teaching children about the joys of reading. Nola lives with her husband, Adam, and her two dogs, Yaro and Lulu. When not drawing, writing, reading, playing with her dogs, or teaching, she enjoys gardening. *Hurry Up, Ilua!* is her first book.

Toronto • Iqaluit
www.inhabitmedia.com